Incredible Animal Tales

by

C.L. Keyworth

Watermill Press

Printed in the United States of America

Illustrations by Thomas Heggie

ISBN 0-89375-799-3

Contents

Autumn's Race

Very quietly, Andy Arnold led Autumn out of the stable. Autumn was a big brown horse with a glossy coat. She gave a small whinny, glad to be out in the fresh morning air. She was saddled and ready to ride.

Andy's mother and father were still

asleep, but Grady the cat and Chumley the dog were up. Chumley circled the horse's legs, panting happily. Grady only stretched and yawned—horses bored her.

"Stay, Chumley," Andy said. "We're going too far for you to follow today. Autumn and I are going up to Black Mountain."

An old lumber trail ran along the top of Black Mountain. The trail was packed dirt, about the width of a small road. From there you could see the whole valley and the town of Frostburg.

Autumn liked to amble along the trail, sniffing the morning breezes. But this morning, her ears suddenly perked up. Then Andy heard it, too—the galloping thump of another horse!

Andy turned Autumn toward the noise. There was a blur of black, white, and orange as they were both nearly

*Grady only stretched and yawned—
horses bored her.*

knocked off the trail.

"Hey!" Andy yelled. "You're not alone up here, you know!"

The blur turned into a small black-and-white horse, and on top of the horse sat a girl in an orange jacket. She wasn't very big, but she was about Andy's age.

She brought her horse to a halt. "Whoa, whoa, Betsy!" she said. "I'm sorry, but I didn't see you. There's usually nobody up here."

"Nobody?" Andy said angrily. "Autumn and I come up here all the time."

"I don't see how that can be," the girl said. "I'm up here racing Betsy every morning."

"Racing *her*?" Andy said, looking at the small horse.

"Betsy's small, but she's very fast," the girl said firmly.

"I'll bet!" Andy laughed.

"She is, and I'll prove it," the girl said. "Let's race down to the end of the trail."

"Your runt against my big, beautiful Autumn?" Andy asked.

"Yes!" the girl said.

"You're on!" Andy cried.

They were off. The horses kicked up clouds of leaves behind them. Autumn ran quickly, but she wasn't as quick as Betsy, and the little horse easily beat Autumn.

"Autumn isn't used to running this trail," Andy explained. "She's used to taking it easy."

"O.K., I'll give you and Autumn another chance," the girl declared. "What do you say to a *real* race—from the beginning of the trail to the end?"

"That's over a mile!" Andy exclaimed. But he couldn't resist the challenge. "When should we have this race?"

"How about two weeks from today?" she replied.

"I'll need to work my horse on this trail," Andy said. "And it has to be when you're not here."

"You can have the trail every other day," she said. "Is it a deal?"

"It's a deal. I'll see you here two weeks from today," Andy said.

The girl and her horse jogged off into the woods. "Seven o'clock sharp!" she yelled over her shoulder.

Andy liked the idea of a race. All the way home, he talked to Autumn. He knew the horse could understand him.

"Autumn," Andy said, "you're the fastest racehorse in Frost County. Trust me, Autumn. You can beat that sawed-off excuse for a horse!"

To himself, Andy had to admit that Betsy did seem to be in good condition,

"Seven o'clock sharp!" the girl yelled
over her shoulder.

but he didn't mention this to Autumn.

So, Autumn's training began. Every other day, Andy took her up to race on Black Mountain. And on the days when they weren't up on the ridge, Andy took Autumn around the field in back of his house. He tried to imagine himself as a jockey, light as a feather on Autumn's back.

And all the time, he talked to Autumn. "You're a winner," he whispered in her shiny brown ear. "You're the fastest."

Victory seemed very easy for Andy and his big, beautiful Autumn.

On the day of the race, Andy was very nervous. He could barely eat a piece of toast.

He and Autumn rode up Black Mountain. When they arrived at the starting point, the girl and Betsy were already there.

"Hi!" the girl called. Betsy was pawing the ground as if she were ready to start. "Are you ready?" the girl asked Andy.

"I'm ready," he replied.

"On your mark! Get set! GO!" the girl cried.

The horses flew off, and Andy felt a sudden rush of cool air. He leaned forward in the saddle, whispering into Autumn's ear, "You're the greatest. You're the best. You're the fastest."

Betsy and Autumn were neck and neck. The two horses took the turns with ease and skimmed over the trail.

Then, without warning, Autumn lost her stride. Later, Andy could not clearly remember what happened. Perhaps a bird flew past or, down in the valley, a dog barked. At any rate, Autumn slowed down, and Betsy leaped ahead.

Andy kicked Autumn's sides a bit

harder than he meant to. But this merely surprised Autumn and didn't make her go faster.

Betsy reached the finish a full length ahead of Autumn.

All four of them—the riders and the horses—were panting for breath.

"Thanks for the race," the girl said brightly. "That was fun!"

Sure, thought Andy, *fun for you.* He was so angry he could hardly speak. As he muttered good-by and turned Autumn toward home, he could feel the girl's eyes on his back.

When he knew the girl couldn't hear him, Andy said to Autumn, "That runt beat you! And a girl, too!" He knew these were mean thoughts, but he was in a mean mood.

Things went on like this for a week. Andy fed and cleaned Autumn, but he didn't talk to her, and he didn't ride her. He could see Autumn was hurt. She didn't know what she had done. *You lost, that's what*, Andy thought bitterly. *You lost.*

One morning, Andy had just fed Autumn. He was coming out of the stable when he saw Betsy and the girl.

The girl rode up to him. She didn't bother to say hello. "I don't suppose you'd like my opinion," the girl said.

"About what?" Andy asked.

"About the awful way you're treating Autumn," the girl replied. "I got Betsy when she was just a colt. Right from the start, she was a racer. She just loves to race. It's in her blood, I guess. So I work with her and race her. Someday I'll race her at the state fair or somewhere."

"So what?" said Andy.

"So, your Autumn is not a racer," she

*Andy was coming out of the stable when
he saw Betsy and the girl.*

said. "It doesn't mean she's not a fine horse. I can see that she is. But she's more slow-paced. She likes to enjoy life, take it easy. Am I right?"

"I guess so," Andy admitted.

"I could see you were mad at Autumn for losing the race," the girl said. "But you should like her for what she is."

Andy had to admit that the girl was right. "You certainly speak your mind," he added.

"I guess I do," said the girl. She looked up at Andy and smiled. "By the way, my name is Rosalind, but my friends call me Rosie."

"Hello, Rosie," Andy said. "I'm Andy. I'm sorry that I behaved so foolishly. You're right. Autumn really is a good horse. Maybe you and Betsy would care to take a ride with us today."

"I'd like that a lot, Andy," Rosie

17

replied. Twenty minutes later, Andy and Rosie were riding the trail on Black Mountain.

Andy leaned over and whispered in Autumn's ear, "You're a winner, old girl."

Clopping happily along, Autumn sniffed the air.

Incident at Wild Pond

Andy had a secret. He wouldn't share it with anyone, not even his friend, Rosie — not yet, anyway.

One afternoon, Rosie came by, riding her horse Betsy. She wanted to go for a ride with Andy and his horse Autumn. But Andy's mother, Mrs. Arnold, told her that Andy had been out all after-noon.

"He's been disappearing for hours at a time," said Mrs. Arnold.

This made Rosie suspicious. So the next time she saw Andy, she talked to him about it. "Where have you been going?" she asked. "Your mother says you're out for hours lately. It sounds mysterious."

"Not at all," replied Andy. "I've just been tramping around Black Mountain, that's all."

And that was true. What Andy didn't tell Rosie was that he had found a special, secret place. When he was ready, he'd show Rosie the place and surprise her.

The place was a pond way back in the woods on Black Mountain. Andy called it Wild Pond, because there was so much wildlife there. The pond was a deep blue color and was fringed with white birch trees.

Andy stumbled onto the pond by accident one day as he was taking a walk. There were birds singing in the trees and chipmunks rustling in the undergrowth. On the pond, a mother duck swam with her ten ducklings, while the water's surface was occasionally broken by the sleek bodies of two otters.

Andy sat there quietly for about half an hour and was just about to leave when he heard a noise behind him. Coming out of the woods toward the pond was a young deer, about a year old. The yearling was reddish brown, had lost his spots, and was just sprouting new, nubby horns. He didn't see Andy and went down to the pond to drink. Then he turned and went back into the woods.

*On the pond, a mother duck swam with
her ten ducklings.*

The yearling was beautiful, so slender and graceful. Right away, Andy decided he wanted to take the deer's picture. His parents had given him a camera for his birthday only a month before. *What a great photograph this would be,* Andy thought.

The very next day, Andy was back at Wild Pond, and he had his camera with him. It wasn't big or expensive, but it would do. Andy waited patiently, and finally the yearling appeared. But the young deer was too far away to photograph. Andy tried to move closer, but his pants caught on a branch. The branch broke with a loud snap, and the yearling turned and bounded off, his white tail in the air.

Andy went back every day for several weeks. Some days, the yearling never showed up. On the days when he did appear, he was too far away for Andy to photograph him. Andy liked Wild Pond and he liked just seeing the deer, but he was determined to get a picture.

Andy borrowed some books on nature from the library and read about white-tailed deer. One book said that deer liked salt and would travel a long way to get to a salt lick. That was it! Andy decided he would make a salt lick.

That night, he poured two boxes of salt into a bowl and added enough water to make it harden. The next day, he took this homemade salt lick to Wild Pond and put it on an old stump of a tree.

Soon, the yearling was coming regularly to the salt lick. Andy waited closer and closer to the tree stump. After a few days, he would sit several feet from the lick, and the yearling would come right up without minding. He only looked at

Andy with the flick of an eye. Andy could take as many photographs as he wanted.

That was when Andy decided to tell Rosie his secret. "Wear your hiking boots," he told her. "We're going far back into Black Mountain."

"Won't you tell me where we're going?" Rosie asked as they trudged through the woods.

"You'll see," Andy said. He was very pleased with himself and couldn't wait for Rosie to see the deer.

When they got to Wild Pond, Rosie let out a little gasp. "Oh, Andy," she said. "It's great. Everything is so still and beautiful."

"You haven't seen anything yet," he told her as they sat down a few yards away from the salt lick. Andy didn't tell her anything about what she would be seeing. He just told her to wait.

After a while, the yearling appeared. He picked his way over the forest floor, his coat shining red-brown where the sun hit it. Andy and Rosie watched as he got closer and closer. Finally, the deer got to the salt lick. He looked at Andy and Rosie without concern, then began to lick contentedly at the salt.

Andy glanced at Rosie. But her look of amazement had given way to a frown. After the yearling had drunk at the pond and gone back to the woods, Rosie exploded.

"Andy," she cried. "Did you put up that salt lick?"

"Yes," he said. "Why, what's wrong?"

"Don't you know?" Rosie asked. "Setting out a salt lick is the last thing you should have done."

"I don't get it," Andy replied.

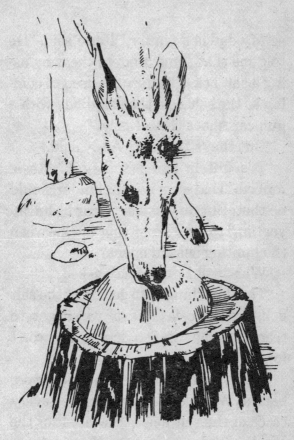

The deer began to lick contentedly at the salt.

"My dad is a hunter," Rosie said. "He told me that some hunters cheat by using a salt lick. The deer get used to coming to the salt lick, then anybody with a gun can shoot them easily. "

"But that's not fair," Andy said.

"It's unfair and it's illegal," Rosie replied. "Dad says no real hunter would do that. But do you want your beautiful yearling to be a—a sitting duck—when the hunting season opens?"

"What will I do?" Andy asked.

"The first thing is to get rid of the salt lick," said Rosie. "Next, we've got to teach the yearling a lesson he won't forget."

The next day, Rosie and Andy were back at Wild Pond. They removed every trace of the salt lick and waited for the yearling to come down to the pond.

"I suppose we have to do this," Andy

said. "But my heart isn't in it."

"I know," said Rosie. "Mine isn't, either."

At last, the yearling came poking through the brush.

"Ready?" asked Andy.

"Yes," said Rosie.

The yearling came closer. Suddenly, Andy and Rosie jumped up.

"Hey!" yelled Rosie.

"*Whooo!*" yelled Andy.

Yelling and clapping their hands, they ran toward the deer.

For a second, the yearling stared at them. He didn't look afraid, merely surprised. Then he leaped in the air, lifted his white tail like a flag, and was gone in an instant.

"Do you think he'll be afraid of humans now?" Andy asked.

"I hope so," Rosie said. "But I sure

*Yelling and clapping their hands, Andy and
Rosie ran toward the deer.*

hated to do that."

"I know, but it was the right thing to do," Andy said with a sigh. He looked out over Wild Pond.

"Hey!" Rosie cried in a low whisper. "What's that?" She pointed to two dark shapes in the pond.

"The otters!" Andy said. "I forgot to tell you about the otters."

Andy started to get out his camera, and then he paused. "Let's just watch them," he said.

So Andy and Rosie sat down quietly in the stillness of Wild Pond, as the otters bobbed and weaved like dancers in the water.

The Puppy Walker's Lesson

"Dad, listen to this," Andy Arnold said to his father, who was stretched out on the couch. "Here's a newspaper story about a place that trains guide dogs for the blind. They want volunteers—they call them Puppy Walkers—to raise the puppies until they're a year old."

Mr. Arnold opened one eye and then closed it. "No," he said.

"Think of what I'd learn," Andy continued. "Think of the good I could do! Think of the fun of raising the puppy!"

"Son," said Mr. Arnold, "I wish you took an interest in stamp collecting—something quiet."

"They want people who have already raised dogs," said Andy, "and I've already raised Chumley." Chumley was Andy's mutt.

"I could get you a model airplane kit," Mr. Arnold said hopefully.

"I like animals," Andy insisted.

"I know," sighed Mr. Arnold. "And I know I'll say yes to the puppy." He shut both eyes firmly.

So Andy brought home Jewel. Jewel was a ten-week-old golden retriever. She

"I could get you a model airplane kit,"
Mr. Arnold said hopefully.

had beautiful red-gold hair and big, puppy feet. Everybody loved her, even Mr. Arnold.

Ms. Hatch, the supervisor of the Puppy Walker program, visited the Arnolds. She explained that it was important for the whole family to become involved in Jewel's training. But it was Andy who was to be mostly responsible for her care.

Mrs. Arnold asked, "Do we have to teach Jewel how to be a guide dog for a sightless person?"

"Oh, no," said Ms. Hatch. "We'll do that when you return her after a year. All you must teach her is basic obedience."

"I should teach her to answer to her name?" asked Andy. "And to sit and to stay?"

"That's right," Ms. Hatch said. "I know you'll take good care of her." She said good-by, telling them she'd be back every six weeks to see how Jewel was doing.

That night, Andy fixed up a place in the cellar for Jewel. He put down newspapers in one spot and put an old towel in a box. Jewel curled up in the box and began chewing on the towel.

The next morning, Andy and Chumley went down to see how Jewel was. The puppy jumped up and down so hard when she saw them, she kept falling down. Andy sat down and gathered her in his arms.

Then Chumley sat there looking at Andy as if to say, "What about old friends?" So Andy grabbed Chumley, too.

Jewel learned easily and well. She seemed to know she would someday be of service. She wanted to please Andy.

*Jewel curled up in the box and began chewing
on the towel.*

By the time she was three months old, she knew all the basic commands.

Andy took her everywhere so she'd get used to different places, smells, and noises. On Saturday afternoons, he'd often take her to the train station. At first, the churning engine of the train scared her. But soon she sat obediently, despite the tooting horn and clicking wheels.

Andy also took her to busy city streets and shopping malls where there were lots of people. He knew she had to learn to be comfortable in crowds and not be distracted.

Meanwhile, Jewel was growing up. Her fat, puppy shape had lengthened into the lean lines of the retriever. "She's finally growing into her feet," Mrs. Arnold observed.

At the same time, Andy was growing

more and more fond of the dog. In fact, the thought of giving her up had become unbearable. He loved Jewel! He knew she wasn't his, not really. She belonged to somebody in the future, a sightless man or woman. For that person, she would be eyes to see the whole world.

But Andy felt that Jewel really belonged to him. He didn't want to give her up. Yet, he didn't tell his feelings to anyone.

One day, Andy's father said, "I'll sure miss Jewel when she's gone."

"She won't miss us," Andy replied gruffly. But he didn't believe it.

At last, the year was up. The evening before Andy had to return Jewel, he took her for a walk after dinner. The two of them went up into the woods on Black Mountain.

Andy wished he and Jewel could just

*Andy wished he and Jewel could just
keep walking.*

keep walking. Maybe they could run away together, and then he wouldn't have to take her back. The more he thought of running away, the more he became lost in thought. And as he got lost in thought, he also got lost in the woods.

Somehow, Andy had gone too far. He thought he knew Black Mountain pretty well, but now he was confused. The last light was fading from the big pine trees. Suddenly, it was dark.

"I'm glad I brought along a flashlight, Jewel," Andy said. But when he turned the light on, nothing happened. He shook the light, and it flared dimly before going out for good. They were in blackness. There was going to be a full moon, but it hadn't risen yet.

Andy started to walk in what he thought was the right direction. But after ten minutes of crashing through the underbrush, Andy was even more lost than before.

Blackness. *So this is what it's like,* Andy thought. He couldn't even see his hand in front of his face. *I might as well be blind,* he said to himself.

Andy crouched down next to Jewel. His heart was pounding, but he was thinking clearly. "Now I see why I've got to give you up, Jewel. For somebody who lives in this darkness all the time, you're going to be a wonderful gift."

Andy and Jewel sat in the forest and waited for the moon to rise. When it did, it was full and golden and bright. It gave enough light so that Andy and Jewel could get home.

The next day, Andy delivered Jewel to Ms. Hatch. She had given him a bouncing puppy, and he was bringing back a well-behaved young dog, ready for formal training. Andy was proud of himself.

He was also proud that he felt no regrets when Ms. Hatch led Jewel away. But he had already said his good-bys the night before, in the dark forest on Black Mountain.

"You know, Andy," Ms. Hatch said when she returned, "we like Puppy Walkers to bring in a dog and take another puppy right away. We always need good Puppy Walkers."

"Another dog, Ms. Hatch?" Andy asked. "I don't know."

"I've got a beautiful black Labrador retriever," Ms. Hatch said. "Won't you look at her?"

When Andy returned home that afternoon with Jet, the black Labrador, his father was stretched out on the couch

43

with his eyes closed. He opened one eye, looked at Jet, and closed it.

"Nice dog," said Mr. Arnold. "I don't suppose it's a stamp collection in disguise, is it?"

The Man Who Told Stories

Old Man Cross lived on the back side of Black Mountain. Many people thought he was a mean-tempered old hermit. The fact was that Mr. Cross just liked being alone. But it was different with Andy Arnold. Andy was Mr. Cross's friend.

Andy liked to bring up vegetables from his mother's garden to exchange for Mr. Cross's homemade honey and jams. When Andy came to visit, Mr. Cross would serve some tea. Then the two of them would chat. *Mr. Cross has been everywhere and seen everything,* Andy thought. *He has lots of stories to tell.*

One afternoon, Mr. Cross and Andy were sharing a pot of tea. Mr. Cross was talking about bears.

"Whenever you go out berrying, take along a metal pie pan. Bears love berries, you know," Mr. Cross told Andy. "If you bang that pan a few times, you'll scare the bears away."

"Have you ever met a bear?" Andy asked.

"Sure," Mr. Cross replied. "I was almost eaten by a grizzly bear once!"

When Andy came to visit, Mr. Cross would serve some tea.

"No!" cried Andy.

"On my life!" said Mr. Cross. "Take my advice, Andy. If you ever meet a grizzly, play dead. Just fall down as if you were gone. Then he'll leave you alone."

"That must take courage," Andy said.

"It takes nerves of steel," Mr. Cross said modestly. "I used to have a picture of a grizzly I killed up in Alaska. I guess I've misplaced it."

When Andy came home to dinner that night, Mr. Arnold said, "Play dead, huh? It sounds impossible."

"I know I'd want to run if I met up with a grizzly bear," said Mrs. Arnold, "or any bear," she added.

"Sure, but if you ran, you'd be caught," said Andy. "When you think about it, Mr. Cross's advice is good."

"His stories are just tall tales, Andy,"

concluded Mr. Arnold.

"Maybe," agreed Andy. "But they're entertaining."

The next time Andy paid Mr. Cross a visit, the old man told him about his pet mockingbird.

"I had a real terrific bird named Carrie," Mr. Cross said. "She could talk, you know. She could say anything at all."

"I knew mockingbirds could imitate sounds," said Andy. "I didn't know they could say words."

"My Carrie could," said Mr. Cross. "She'd ask for something to eat like this." He squeezed his voice into a bird-like sound and said, "*Cheese! Cheese!* And she could say my name as clear as a bell. *Mr. Cross*, she'd say."

"That's amazing," Andy said.

"Oh, she was a rascal," Mr. Cross said. "I lost her though."

"How?" Andy asked.

"She got out of her cage and flew off one day," Mr. Cross said. "She flew into the woods."

"Did you ever find her again?"

"I saw her a year later!" Mr. Cross said. "I was taking a walk in the woods when I heard, *Mr. Cross! Mr. Cross!* It was her, you see."

"Did you take her home with you then?" Andy asked.

"No. We had a little visit, then she took off again," said Mr. Cross. "I guess she preferred the freedom of the wild wood."

The story of Carrie, the talking mockingbird, was greeted with disbelief by Andy's mother and father.

"Take it with a grain of salt," Mr. Arnold advised.

"A salt shaker's worth," his mother

added. "He's a nice old fellow, Andy. But maybe he's gotten a bit confused after living alone all this time."

A few weeks later, Andy and his dog Chumley were taking a walk up on Black Mountain. Andy had many happy memories of Black Mountain. Here, he had often ridden his horse Autumn, and here he had once discovered a secret pond.

Andy was so absorbed in his memories, he didn't notice that Chumley was far ahead of him. Suddenly, he realized that his dog was growling at something. When he caught up with Chumley, he discovered the object of Chumley's interest — a skunk.

"No!" Andy shouted at Chumley. "Come away!"

But Chumley was very excited by this neatly striped little animal. He seemed to think it was his duty to growl the fellow down.

"It's a skunk, Chumley," said Andy, ready to flee at any moment. "Heel!"

Meanwhile, the skunk was looking at Chumley with disdain. Andy remembered what Mr. Cross had once told him about skunks. Mr. Cross said that skunks were the most fearless creatures in the world because they had the best weapon.

Just then, Chumley's growl turned into a bark. The skunk began to stamp its feet. Mr. Cross had also told Andy that skunks stamped their feet when they got mad. And this one was doing just that!

Then the skunk did an amazing thing. It stood on its hands with its tail straight up in the air and peered at Chumley through its front legs.

*The skunk stood on its hands with its tail
straight up in the air.*

"This is it!" Andy said, and began to run. Skunks, Mr. Cross had told him, did handstands before they released their spray. Andy hadn't believed it at the time.

"Chumley, come on!" Andy shouted over his shoulder as he ran.

After Andy had run a good distance, he sat down, caught his breath, and began calling for Chumley.

Soon, Chumley appeared. The poor creature was rolling over and over in the underbrush. He smelled powerfully of skunk.

"Oh, Chum," Andy sighed. "You smell worse than anything on earth."

Chumley stopped his agonized rolling for a moment. He looked at Andy with sadder, but wiser, eyes. He seemed to be asking, "What's going to happen to me?"

"I don't know what to do with you,"

Andy said, as if the question had been spoken. "If you were an article of clothing, you'd have to be burned. Of course, we won't burn you," he added quickly. "Come along," he told Chumley. "We'll go ask Mr. Cross."

Chumley followed Andy at a distance, whimpering and rubbing his nose in the dirt at every opportunity.

When they got to Mr. Cross's cabin, Andy told him the story. He pointed to his outcast dog.

"What can I do?" he asked. "I know it's going to be impossible to clean him up."

"Let me think," Mr. Cross said. He disappeared into his house. When he came back, he was holding a small, black book.

"It's my diary," he explained. "I remember meeting a skunk back in '48. Now, what did I do? Ah, here it is." He read for a moment and then looked at Andy triumphantly.

"Tomato juice!" he declared.

"Tomato juice?" Andy asked.

"Tomato juice," Mr. Cross repeated firmly. "Rub him down with plenty of it, then wash him off. He'll be his old sweet-smelling self again." He added, muttering, "If dogs can ever be said to be sweet-smelling."

It turned out that Mr. Cross was right. Andy doused poor Chumley with a case of tomato juice. When he'd rinsed him off, Chumley smelled like a dog again. For a few months, he smelled like skunk whenever he got wet, but generally he was tolerable.

The Arnolds were impressed.

"I'll never doubt the old man again," said Mr. Arnold.

That was how Andy felt. After that,

*Andy doused poor Chumley with a case
of tomato juice.*

whenever Andy went up the back side of Black Mountain to pay a visit to Mr. Cross, he just put his feet up and listened happily.

"Did I ever tell you about Frieda, the dancing chicken?" Mr. Cross asked him one day.

"No, tell me about it," Andy replied.

"I used to have a picture of her," Mr. Cross began, "but I guess I've misplaced it."

The Nest in General Apple's Hat

Andy Arnold was sitting on a park bench. It was a bright, sunny afternoon in early July. Andy had stretched out his long legs and was whistling. He was watching the mayor clean the bronze statue of General Apple. General Apple was the Revolutionary War hero who had won the famous Battle of Frostburg.

Every Fourth of July, the mayor gave a rousing speech in front of General Apple's statue. His speech was followed by a picnic, and later, there were fireworks. So every year, the mayor liked to spruce up General Apple.

Andy stopped whistling when he heard the mayor exclaim, "Whoa!"

Andy walked over to the statue. The mayor had pulled himself up onto the general and was looking into the general's broad-brimmed hat.

"Hello, Andy," said the mayor. "Now this is the oddest thing—there's a nest up here, right in the general's hat."

Andy climbed up beside the mayor. Sure enough, there was a little nest in one fold of the hat. Inside the nest were six white eggs, speckled with brown.

"It's the nest of a house wren," said Andy. "The mother must have flown off when we climbed up here."

"Well, the nest will have to be removed," the mayor said.

"No," cried Andy, "that will hurt the eggs!"

"There are no two ways about it," the mayor said. "The statue has to be in top shape for the Fourth of July."

"A little wren's nest won't hurt anything," Andy said.

"A little nest, you say?" cried the mayor. "That mess of sticks and twigs right over the general's left eye? No, it absolutely will not do!"

Andy and the mayor climbed down, and they saw the house wren return to her nest. She was small and quick and brown.

"Andy, you know all about birds and

"The nest will have to be removed,"
the mayor said.

animals," said the mayor. "I'll put you in charge of the nest. Maybe it can be moved. See what you can do."

Andy visited the library that afternoon and looked through several books about birds, but he read nothing which said a nest could be safely moved.

The next day, Andy went to see the mayor. "The wren and her nest cannot be moved," Andy explained, "but I have discovered a reason why she should stay."

"Let's hear it," the mayor said reluctantly.

"Did you know that wrens played an important role in the Battle of Frostburg?"

"No, did they?" The mayor sounded surprised.

"Certainly," said Andy. "General Apple himself used them as messengers.

They would fly over enemy territory with a message in their little beaks. They dodged bullets easily."

"Amazing," said the mayor. "How did they know where to go?"

"General Apple trained them himself," Andy said. "The wrens were full of patriotic spirit."

"Amazing," the mayor repeated. "In fact, it's hard to believe."

"Yes," admitted Andy, "that's the problem. It's unbelievable—and completely untrue."

"Andy," said the mayor sternly, "find a way to move the nest!"

The next day, Andy reported to the mayor again. "The wren and her nest cannot be moved," said Andy. "But I have discovered a new fact about wrens."

The mayor looked suspicious.

"You look suspicious, sir," said Andy. "But hear me out. General Apple was a bird watcher. On the morning of the Battle of Frostburg, he got up early, hoping to catch sight of a bird."

"What sort of bird?" asked the mayor. "Was it a house wren, by any chance?"

"Exactly, sir," said Andy. "He was looking for the small, but beautiful, house wren. What he saw instead were enemy troops advancing. His early start saved the day."

There was silence while the mayor looked at Andy. "Tsk, tsk," said the mayor. "More stories."

"I call it creative history," Andy said.

"I can think of better terms," said the mayor. "Lying, for example. Now go off, Andy, and find a practical solution to this problem. The Fourth of July is tomorrow."

That evening, Andy went into the city park to look at the wren and her nest. When he climbed up on the statue, the little wren flew to a nearby tree where she made soft, worried sounds and hopped around. In one hand, Andy had a shoe box. He thought he would make one attempt to move the nest.

Carefully, he cupped one hand around the nest with its six eggs. But right away, he saw the problem. The nest was made so that its walls were supported by the general's hat. If Andy moved the nest, it would collapse.

Just then, the wren flew up to Andy. She didn't attack him as other mother birds might have done. She merely sat on the general's shoulder and looked at Andy. She cocked her head as if to say, "Why are you doing this?" Andy didn't have an answer.

*The wren sat on the general's shoulder and
looked at Andy.*

The next morning, Andy walked into town for the Fourth of July celebrations. First, he checked on the nest, and then he went to see the mayor. Today, the mayor was writing his speech.

"The wren and her nest cannot be moved," Andy said.

"No more stories," cried the mayor.

"I have no more stories," Andy said, flinging himself into a chair. "There is nothing to be said in defense of the wren! She's useless! No good!"

"She is?" asked the mayor.

"Is she patriotic?" asked Andy.

"No," said the mayor.

"Is she smart?" asked Andy. "Is she useful?"

"No," agreed the mayor.

"There you have it," said Andy. "She's worthless. Destroy the nest!"

Even the mayor looked somewhat

downcast at Andy's words.

"Of course," said Andy, with a sideways look at the mayor, "she *is* one thing."

"What?" asked the mayor.

"A symbol," said Andy.

"A symbol?" asked the mayor.

"That wren and her nest stand for something else," Andy replied. "By the way, the eggs are hatching this very minute, sir."

"Hatching? Oh, dear," said the mayor.

"Yes," said Andy. "And don't those six newborn birds stand for the newborn America? Isn't the Fourth of July really America's birthday?"

"Yes," cried the mayor. "It is! Andy, I'd like to use that in my speech."

"Be my guest," said Andy. "And won't it be great to have the wren and her nest right there while you're making your speech?"

So Andy saved the wren and her nest. And so it happened that six baby wrens came into the world in General Apple's hat. The mayor made his rousing speech. If the wrens had been listening as they pecked their way out of their shells, they might have been surprised at the mayor's words.

"These birds are a symbol!" the mayor declared, pointing at the mess of sticks and twigs.

Andy sat on the grass and munched an apple as he listened to the mayor's speech. He was wondering if he might be a politician when he grew up.

The Blizzard Goat

Andy Arnold loved animals. "He's crazy about them," his mother would say with a mixture of pride and regret. In other ways, Andy was a typical sixteen-year-old. He liked pizza, baseball, and old movies on television.

But he was crazy about animals. He loved his horse Autumn, his dog Chumley, and Grady the cat. In the past, he had also loved four hamsters, a flock of chickens, and a pet snake. In the past, Mr. and Mrs. Arnold had been patient.

But now they were feeling very impatient. The three Arnolds were in the backyard, looking at Andy's newest pet.

"Isn't she beautiful?" Andy asked. "Look at her little black hooves and her little beard!"

"Look at her big, wicked teeth," said Mrs. Arnold.

They were all looking at a goat, a small, brown nanny goat. Her name, Andy said, was Sookie.

"Goats eat things, Andy," Mr. Arnold said, "like flowers in flower gardens and clothes on clotheslines."

Sookie looked at the Arnolds with an

*Sookie looked at the Arnolds with
an air of boredom.*

air of boredom and began to nibble Mr. Arnold's pants leg.

"Goats also eat grass," Andy said. "She'll keep the backyard mowed all summer long."

"What will she do in winter?" Andy's mother asked.

"Summer and winter, she'll give milk," Andy explained.

"Goat's milk," said Mr. Arnold. "Somewhat flavored of goat, I'll bet."

"It's very good for you," Andy insisted.

So Sookie came to live with the Arnolds. In June, Andy staked her out in their big backyard, and she kept the grass closely cropped.

There were one or two difficult times. Once, Sookie ate half the garden hose. Another time, she tried to eat Grady the cat. Fortunately, Grady woke up in time.

On the brighter side, Sookie grew

especially fond of Mr. Arnold. She liked to follow him around whenever he was in the backyard.

Sookie was happy all summer long, munching grass and giving milk. But when cooler weather arrived, Sookie became restless. She didn't seem to like the cold. By November, she refused to go outside at all. She just stayed in the barn.

But she didn't like being pent up any better than she liked being cold. She grew cranky. She took to bleating loud and long to show her unhappiness. The sound of her miserable *baaa*s could often be heard, day and night.

"Sookie was bleating at four in the morning," Mr. Arnold said over breakfast one day. "Four o'clock in the morning is a bad time to be awakened by a goat."

"I know," Andy admitted. Her bleating had even gotten on Andy's nerves, and he was crazy about animals.

In December, Mr. Arnold went to Elm City on a business trip. The day he left was clear and crisp, but the next morning, the whole world had turned white. A steady snow was coming down. It snowed all morning and all afternoon. By nightfall, snowdrifts were building up around the house.

"Mom," Andy said, "the radio says there are cars stranded on highways all over the state. I'm going to go see if anybody is out on the road next to our house."

"Be careful," said Mrs. Arnold. "Just go to the top of the hill and look down."

When Andy returned, his cheeks were bright red with the cold. "They're down there all right," he said. "I can see the

*By nightfall, snowdrifts were building up
around the house.*

lights of four cars by the side of the road."

"It's below freezing outside," said his mother. "It's dangerous for them."

"I've got to go down and get them," said Andy. "If Dad were here, he'd do it."

"You could get down there, but how would you get back?" Mrs. Arnold asked. "It's completely dark, and it's still snowing. You'll get lost between here and the road."

"Sookie!" Andy cried.

"Sookie?" asked his mother.

"Goats have a perfect sense of direction," Andy replied. "Shepherds use goats to bring home their flocks of sheep, don't they? Sookie can lead us back here."

"I hope you're right," said Mrs. Arnold.

Andy put on a suit of long underwear, an extra pair of socks, two sweaters, a jacket and a ski mask. He also grabbed a flashlight.

He went to get Sookie in the barn and tied a long rope to her collar. But the goat wouldn't budge.

"We're going to save people, Sookie," Andy said. "We're going on a dangerous mission in a blizzard! We're going to be brave!"

Sookie was not impressed. She planted her four feet on the floor and glared at Andy.

"Sorry, old girl," Andy said, as he dragged Sookie out of the barn and into the snow. He continued dragging her through the snow and up the hill.

When they went over the crest of the hill, Andy lost sight of the house. Everything was dark and snowy. His only guides were the red lights of the cars.

"We're going to be brave," Andy kept

repeating, under his breath.

It was difficult trudging through the snow, and Sookie wasn't giving Andy any help. She began to bleat like a fog-horn off a lonely coast.

At last, Andy reached the first car. Inside it were a man and his wife and their two little girls.

"Thank heavens," said the man. "We didn't want to spend the night out here!"

The family bundled up as best they could. Each of the adults carried a child and took hold of Sookie's rope.

"Now, Sookie, do it!" Andy said. "Lead us home!"

And Sookie did. In fact, she was so glad to be going toward home that she bounded through the snow. She knew exactly where she was going. She took them right through the snow at a gallop. In no time, everyone had reached Andy's

Sookie bounded through the snow.

house safely.

But when it was time for Andy and Sookie to go back down to the other cars, Sookie balked again. She began to bleat. Again, Andy dragged her through the snow.

They made three more trips, with Sookie bleating unhappily all the way down, and bounding happily back up again. In this manner, Andy and Sookie saved a minister and his wife, a young man, and a mother with her small child.

"You didn't want to do it," Andy told Sookie as he rubbed her down in the barn. "But you did it! You're a hero, goat!"

Inside the house, Mrs. Arnold was making a huge pot of chili. The minister pitched in by making a delicious batch of cornbread. Andy lit a fire in the fireplace, and everyone drank apple cider.

That night, every spare bed, cot and

sleeping bag was used. In the morning, when the roads were cleared, Andy helped the families get back to their cars. There were many heartfelt thanks for the Arnolds and especially for Sookie.

When Mr. Arnold came back the next day, he told Andy how proud he was of him. He even had a kind word for Sookie.

"Long may she bleat!" he declared.

But Sookie was strangely quiet. Nobody knew why, but she had stopped her bleating. Maybe she simply was glad to be safe and sound after her dangerous mission.

That winter, every once in a great while, Sookie would give out a single *Baaa!* Andy thought she just wanted to keep in practice.

Picnic with an Elephant

Andy Arnold was sixteen. He thought he'd had an interesting life, until he camped out one night with an elephant. After that, he figured he'd never be completely surprised by life again. This is what happened.

For many years, the town of Frostburg had its own zoo. Then the zoo closed down. The animals were sent to zoos in different cities. The four elephants were being sent to the Hillstown Zoo. Joe Robbins, the elephant handler, was going with them.

One day, Joe called Andy. Everybody in town knew that Andy was good with animals, and that's just what Joe needed.

"I've got a problem as big as an elephant," said Joe. "In fact, my problem *is* an elephant."

Joe told Andy his story. He'd sent three elephants in three trucks to the Hillstown Zoo. But the fourth truck had broken down. It couldn't be fixed for a week. Joe Robbins had a stalled elephant on his hands.

"I've decided to walk to Hillstown with Mrs. Thompson," said Joe. "Mrs.

T. — that's the elephant."

"But Hillstown is fifty miles away," Andy said.

"I know," said Joe. "But there's nothing else I can do. Mrs. T. can't stay here alone. The question is, will you come along and help me?"

So the next day, Andy found himself hiking down a road with an elephant. Joe led Mrs. T. on a long rope. They traveled on back roads to avoid traffic.

It was a bright spring morning and the sun felt hot on Andy's back.

"Life on the open road!" Andy cried. "Joe, there's nothing like it. What have I been missing all my life?"

At noon, they stopped for lunch by the side of the road. Mrs. T. ate grass while Joe and Andy munched the sandwiches they had packed. After lunch, Andy would have liked a long nap in the warm sun. But they had to move on.

After another two hours of walking, Andy was exhausted. "Isn't Mrs. T. tired?" he asked Joe.

"Elephants have lots of stamina," Joe replied.

So Andy dragged himself up and kept hiking. He tried to imagine he was Admiral Byrd at the South Pole. *What an adventure!* he thought to himself. He wished his friends could see him. But his feet hurt.

At sunset, Joe called a halt. They decided to camp out in an empty field, and they tied Mrs. T. to a tree.

Out of his grub bag, Joe got some dried meat and potatoes. He made a fire and fixed a stew over it. Mrs. T. had a dinner of grass and tree branches.

"This is the life!" cried Andy. "Roughing it, a picnic with an elephant under the

Joe made a fire and fixed a stew.

stars—I love it!" Andy stretched out and watched the fire burn down to embers. He felt wonderful, even though his legs ached from walking so far. He opened his mouth to say something more to Joe, but words turned into a yawn, and he fell fast asleep.

Eight hours later, Andy was dreaming that Mrs. T. was spraying him with water from her trunk. When he woke up, he was soaked to the skin. A warm rain was pouring down. Joe was also drenched. Big drops of water were running off Mrs. T.'s floppy ears.

There was no chance of building a fire and having breakfast. They just had to start walking. Both Joe and Andy had ponchos in their packs, but there was no point in putting them on over soaking clothes. So they trudged along in the rain.

Roughing it isn't all it's cracked up to be, Andy said to himself.

Andy kept thinking of breakfast. He imagined a big plate of flapjacks and bacon. He thought about how cozy it would be inside his own home.

They walked for an hour and the rain let up a little. Few cars passed them, and there were not many houses. The road seemed dreary and deserted. Suddenly, a car screeched to a halt next to them.

The driver shook his head in disbelief when he saw the elephant. But he managed to warn the travelers that the river ahead of them was swelling rapidly. Then he drove off.

"Let's go ahead and see how bad it is," Joe said.

When they reached the river, they saw that a swirling flood had almost submerged a low, stone bridge. Near the bridge, a small group of people had gathered. They were huddled in the rain, looking at the river.

A man left the group and ran toward Joe and Andy.

"I don't know what you're doing with an elephant in a rainstorm," the man said, "but it's just what we need right now. Please help us save my daughter's life!"

Joe and Andy listened to the man's story. His house was by the river. An hour ago, his ten-year-old daughter had fallen into the water. She was swept downstream, but she managed to grab hold of a tree limb and save herself. But the tree was an uprooted one, stuck in the middle of the river.

Joe and Andy peered through the rain. They could see the little girl clinging to

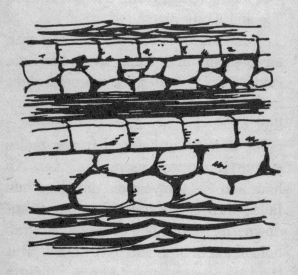

*A swirling flood had almost submerged
a low, stone bridge.*

the trunk of the tree. She was surrounded by swirling grey water.

"Mrs. T. can easily wade into that river," Joe said.

"She can't do it alone, Joe," Andy said. "Let me ride her. I can do it, you'll see."

"O.K., Andy. I'm too old to be climbing on elephants," Joe said. "And Mrs. T. knows you and likes you—that's important with elephants!"

So Andy was hoisted up on top of Mrs. T.'s broad and slippery back. The ground looked a long way off as Andy grabbed hold of the rope around her neck. Then, he gently kicked her sides.

Mrs. T. plunged into the river. Her legs disappeared into the water. Andy hoped she wouldn't stumble on the rocky river bottom.

Mrs. T. seemed to know where to go. She headed right for the tree where the little girl was desperately clinging.

Andy's clothes were heavy with rain-water. His sneakers felt like sponges. He wondered if he would ever get dry again. The whole world was wet and grey.

At last, they reached the little girl. Andy could see that her face was white and frightened, although she was brave-ly holding on. But she was too far away! Andy couldn't reach her. He couldn't even talk to her over the sound of the rushing water.

But Mrs. T. knew what to do. She reached down her long trunk and coiled it around the girl. Very gently, she lifted the girl up and set her next to Andy.

"Bravo, Mrs. T.!" Andy said, and he held on tight to the little girl. From the shore, he heard a cheer of gratitude.

Several hours later, Andy was once again on the road. Thanks to the little

*Mrs. T. reached down her trunk and
coiled it around the girl.*

girl's family, he and Joe were now dry and well fed. The sun had come out again, and Joe was whistling.

When they reached Hillstown later that day, a crowd of cheering people greeted them. News of Mrs. T.'s brave rescue was all over town. Joe and Andy had a police escort to the zoo. There, they released Mrs. T. into the elephant compound with her old friends.

Joe, of course, was staying with his elephants. He said good-by to Andy at the train station.

"Thanks, Joe," Andy said. "I wouldn't have missed this adventure for the world!"

On the train, Andy sank into his seat. He stretched out his legs, and watched the countryside roll past his window.

This is the life! he thought. *Train travel—there's nothing like it!*